DOC...
SCH...
BERNARD...

Illustrated by
Elsie Lennox

WALKER BOOKS
LONDON

For Thinh and Ly Ung
(Boat Girl)

First published 1990 by Julia MacRae Books
as *Boat Girl* and *Getting In*

This edition published 1992 by
Walker Books Ltd, 87 Vauxhall Walk
London SE11 5HJ

Text © 1990 Bernard Ashley
Illustrations © 1990 Elsie Lennox
Cover illustration © 1992 David Frankland

Printed and bound in Great Britain by
Richard Clay Ltd, Bungay, Suffolk

British Library Cataloguing in Publication Data
A catalogue record for this title is available
from the British Library.
ISBN 0-7445-3014-8

MORE STORIES FROM DOCKSIDE SCHOOL

There isn't much that Bernard Ashley doesn't know about inner city junior schools – because he's the headteacher of one! In fact, the drawings of the headteacher in this book were based on him. He's written lots of stories for young readers, many of them like these Dockside School Stories set in south-east London where he lives and works. His books include *Running Scared* (Commended for the Carnegie Medal), *The Country Boy*, *Dodgem* (all three of which were also television serials), *Bad Blood* and *Dockside School Stories*.

More Walker Doubles

CONTENTS

Boat Girl

Getting In

Boat Girl

1

The letter sent home had warned them no-one
went on the School Journey if a parent didn't
come to the briefing. So there they were in the
school hall, grown-up bottoms overlapping the
rims of children's chairs, with just the one sitter
who fitted her seat, and that was Kim Lung. She
had to be there because her father's English wasn't
up to such a meeting where all the details would
be given out. He had to have a translator, even
after all these years. Now he sat there holding
Kim's hand and staring straight ahead, a short
man with young hair, ready to dip his head to hers
when the time came. Kim eased her hand away,
pulled up her already pulled-up socks. She had
come into the row of seats first, was on the wrong
side of him; and she didn't like holding the hand
with the scar on it. Her father let it drop, fingered
the scar as he often did, like someone blind
reading a story in it, while Kim looked up at all

the adults' faces, feeling very out of place, very
small.

The teachers came in and sat behind the trestle
table at the front. Mr Holt, the headteacher,
nodded and smiled, especially at Kim. It was the
look he gave the helpers and the parents, not the
stare he usually gave the children.

Kim took in a long breath of hall air and sat up.
No, feeling *small* wasn't it. She didn't feel small,
she felt short, just miniature: because what she
knew about some things was as much as anybody
sitting there tonight.

"Letters," Mr Holt said. It was near the end
now and even Kim on her chair was
uncomfortable. All the School Journey details had
been given out and whispered in Vietnamese into
her father's ear. It had to be done like this. She

could speak the rare language well and understand it. Although she couldn't read it, it was all they spoke at home. She had to translate everything from school because her father couldn't read more than his name in English. There was never much put on paper at Kim's place.

"Letters."

The important stuff was over. Kim made that little 'don't worry' sign translators do when they aren't going to bother. She could give the whispering a rest for a few minutes.

"Write often," Mr Holt said. "Children get very homesick if they don't get letters. Write any nonsense you want – but keep it cheerful." Mr Holt made his old joke. "Don't send sad stuff about going into their rooms and seeing the empty pillow. And if the cat dies tell them about the budgie instead!"

"What was that?" Kim's father demanded.

"Nothing much – about children feeling bad."

Mr Lung looked at her. "It isn't you feeling bad, it's me. No help for a week!"

And the meeting ended, with Kim only too glad that she didn't have to queue at the table to tell them about any medicines, or about wetting the bed. That was something! But not enough. Why couldn't her dad be the same as the rest?

2

She enjoyed the first night: six of them in a little
room in bunks, miles away in Wales with a
window where you could see the river winding out
of sight. A lot better than the brick wall at the
back of the Granada which her bedroom faced at
home. And a load of laughs they had! Tracy
Sargent in a zip-up sleeping suit which looked like
an outsize babygro. And Wendy Kent not having
enough hands to keep herself private when
she got undressed. It was better than sleeping
alone above the take-away. In loud whispers they
went on about Lee with the ear-ring and a missing
front tooth, the boy they all went silly about. Till
Mrs Winterburn came in for the third time –
really ratty at the last in her dressing gown and
hairnet – and suddenly the air became heavy, and
loud breathing took over from talk. Kim was
probably the last to sleep; she was more used to
late nights than the rest, with the noise

underneath her bedroom at home. She thought of her uncle at the counter and her father in the back, frying, sieving, banging the pans. And then the next she knew, it was day.

They went to the Big Pit, a disused Welsh coal-mine converted into a museum: which was not a line of smart underground show cases, but a real mine where the walls were dirty, the ceilings were low and the floor was uneven and trickled with water. Everyone wore a helmet with a modern Davy lamp, and it was very quiet under the hard hats as they went down in the big caged lift. Down, down, down, lower than going under the Thames tunnel, further down than anyone went up in the tower block lifts. And it was still very quiet as they walked along the 'roads' following their guide, who stooped as he would have had to stoop all the way to the pit face, going to dig coal. And when they were in a remote tunnel between two sets of closed fire doors he stopped, and said in his choky old Welsh voice, "Now turn off your lamps, will you? See for yourselves a drop of total darkness . . ."

The lights went off, each little searchlight on each hard head.

"You never see total darkness, you know. Not on the surface. There's always something, mind. But here you can't see a hand in front of your face. Can you?"

They tried – and they couldn't. The darkness was the blackest of blacks. It was awesome, had everybody silent for a bit, taking it in – with not even the breathing sounds of the night before, but tense shallow breaths. It was a new experience, something to make everyone think: and an instant of time when Kim Lung's mind went suddenly to when she'd heard talk about total darkness before, when she'd heard her father tell of it. Not underground like now, not in the west, but in a Vietnam night of a blackness never known in Britain. She remembered the talk about her mother and her father hiding in the jungle, waiting

with their group of refugees for the men who
would lead them to the mother boat. Twelve of
them from the south who had paid their gold to
the old man in the city, the twelve who had met
up by the sea and gone out in fishing boats to the
island off-shore. She remembered her dad telling

his brother of the moonless, starless darkness which had been so black, like now, that they had had to put their hands on the shoulders in front, so as not to get lost as they were led through the wet and slippery jungle. And how, to be counted by the boat man, they had had to stamp on the ground as they passed a certain spot because he couldn't see them.

And Kim had been there: not to be counted, but big in the total darkness of her mother's womb: knowing it only from what she had heard her father say afterwards.

As if suddenly attacked by a sharp pain, Kim shuddered, and in the dripping blackness of the mine she couldn't help but make the smallest of cries.

The lights came on.

"You all right, my pet? Wouldn't scare you for the world."

"Scaredy-pants!"

But Kim didn't seem to hear what Wendy said. She was shaking off the old, dark thought. That wasn't what she'd come on the School Journey for, to feel bad.

3

By the time they got back to the grey stone house
which was the School Journey Centre, it was time
for the evening meal: all scraping chairs and
passing the water and the clatter of cutlery on
plates. It had been a long day and nobody was too
faddy to leave any of the hot-pot, mash and baked
beans. Whole loaves disappeared like slices and no-
one cleared their mouths to even mention missing
their television. In what had been the dining room
of the country mansion, used to best silver and
cut-glass, Dockside School ate fast: taking the next
mouthful before finishing the last, eyes much
sharper for seconds of food than for the letters
being dished out.

The post had come: a thin pack in a thick
rubber band which had been delivered while they
were down the Big Pit. Not a lot of it, it was only
their second day away, but some children's parents
had thought ahead and got letters and cards off

before the coach had left London.

"Just a few," said Mr Brewer, giving them out. "There'll be another post tomorrow . . ."

Kim watched Wendy open hers: saw her not bothering with the letter so much as the fiver folded up in it. How could she? She watched Joss with his card written in black italic script, laughing at some joke. And she watched Lyndsey sniffing at her pink Snoopy paper with its upside-down triangle of kisses. Then it was Duty Group, and washing up, and Kim was where she always spent a lot of her time – up to the wrists of her rubber gloves in a big kitchen sink, watching the suds.

4

The suds she watched the next day, though, were
of a very different sort. Cold, frothing waves of
them where they crashed in at the foot of the
lifeboat cove. A glinty grey, the sea swelled itself
up almost unseen, the wave shape becoming clear
only at the last, just before it went thundering
over the worn rocks.

The sea. Kim stared at it. She had never seen
much of the sea. Her life had hardly taken her
near it since she'd been born. She was much more
used to the slow old Thames not far from the
take-away – and that was very different to this.
She stood apart and watched the water. She was
held by it, because she knew it, the sea – in her
bones, in her blood, in her soul. She was of the
sea, was a true boat person: because Kim had been
born on the mother boat.

She walked with the others round the lifeboat
which had been designed to be so hard to sink. In
its tight-fitting shed hung with medals and

memorials to brave people, she looked at the powerful and sturdy craft, and she thought about that other one: the frail, overcrowded refugee boat. She thought about it in spite of herself, because she certainly didn't want to: no more than she'd wanted to think about that darkness in the Big Pit, which had started all of this off . . .

She remembered hearing her father telling his brother, when he had himself come to Britain. How he and her mother had been allowed on the mother boat with only the clothes they were wearing, everything else left behind on the island, every unnecessary weight, even the sandals from their feet. They had only been allowed the bottles of cough medicine everyone carried in their teeth, stuff to make them drowsy, to help them pass their difficult journey in sleep.

From high on the Welsh cliffs, Kim watched a small fishing boat bobbing out of the shelter of the cove. She heard the screams of the sea birds, each,

it seemed, with its own individual voice. And inside her head she imagined again the shouts and the screams of the people in the mother boat being told to be quiet by the sailors. Adults packed into the bottom where it was roughest and sickest, the elderly in the middle and the youngest on the top. Parents and their children separated: and with so many clamouring to go, no mother being certain that her child had been allowed to follow on. Names being called, backwards and forwards: shrieks of grief when no answers came, and louder shouts of anger from the sailors. Her father had told his brother about it in a flat voice as though it were a fact of life. And he had thought himself lucky, he'd said, because Hoa had her baby inside her, and people pushed to give her a little more room.

"Ain't you ever seen the sea before?" Lee was next to her: but not acting as rough as his voice. He was staring at the waves, too; and he put a hand on her shoulder.

"Not much," Kim said. And she was pleased he hadn't said it gentle, or she might have wanted to cry: not the point of a School Journey at all.

5

They were late back from the coast that evening
and the warden wasn't pleased about it at all. Mrs
Winterburn never grovelled to anyone, but she did
go red when she saw the woman waiting for them
at the front door. She shouted at the children to
hurry – and she ended up serving the potatoes
herself. So there was no time for the games on the
field and in the woods that they'd been promised.
It was wash up, diaries and bed.

And letters. They had time to get the post given
out. Mr Brewer brought it round proudly as if
he'd written it all himself – a fatter batch tonight
with two rubber bands, one going each way.

The people who had had one the night before
all had another, and most of the rest had one, too.
There were posh-looking letters and tatty-looking
letters; there were long ones and short ones; there
were some with drawings put in by little brothers
and sisters, some with money. Some were in

capital letters all through and didn't keep to the
lines, some were faint and scrawly, and one was
done on a computer. They came on white paper,
on blue paper, on pink and rainbow: they were

torn out, ripped off and crinkly-edged.

And nearly everyone got one. But Lee didn't, nor did Parveen: and neither did Kim.

"Early days," said Mr Brewer. "Tomorrow, eh?"

Kim went to bed, tucked in early, and turned her back on all the rude talk going on. The others thought she was too stuck up, but it wasn't that. She just couldn't forget that sea. She couldn't get out of her mind how that fishing boat in the Welsh cove had gone up and down on the water like a matchstick in her washing-up. She couldn't get out of her head the imaginary picture she had of her mother; imaginary because they hadn't even brought their sandals, let alone a photograph. And she began to get cross at her dad. Here she was, filled with sad thoughts which made her miss him – and he hadn't sent her a letter. All the children except three had heard from their homes, and she had to be one of the three! All of their parents were busy people, it wasn't just him. You could see how a lot of them had had a struggle with their ball-points and the paper. So why couldn't he have tried? It didn't need much. What sort of a father was he?

6

It was good in the back seat of the coach, going to
the farm. Especially for Kim because she wasn't
really a back-seat person: she was much more of
an up-front passenger. She didn't fight for a very
front seat or to sit next to a teacher, but she did
like to be where she could hear what they said,
and look at the things they pointed out. She'd sit
next to anyone – she often had to, because she
wasn't one of those glued to the same partner –
but she was surprised when it was Lee who
shouted, "Come on, Kim – up the back with me!"

And she'd gone. That had surprised her a bit,
too. Wendy went, and Tracy Sargent, and Jimmy
and a couple of others. But it was Lee who made
the fun, the one they really wanted to be with, and
it was Kim who he'd pushed in beside him,
squashed her beside the window.

Wendy didn't like it, that was as clear as a sheet
of cling-film. She mucked about all right, so did

Tracy, and they had a lot of laughs with Lee. But she didn't like it because most of what Lee said went Kim's way. And although they both gave him plenty of room for sliding closer, it was Kim he kept tight-to in the corner.

It was the letters, Kim decided: that was why he was being friendly. She hadn't had one, and he hadn't had one. With Parveen, who was up at the front with Narinder, they were a little band of three: and you did make friends with people who were the same as you. Last year the leavers had done it when they'd been told which secondary schools they were going to. School dinner and sandwich people did it all the time. And right now it was the letters: the not having them. It was a sort of comfort, like her family had, living close to other Vietnamese in London. But whatever the reason, Wendy Kent and Tracy Sargent didn't like it: they didn't like it one bit, staring at each other every time Kim spoke as if they didn't understand a word she said.

They liked the farm more. They forgot the coach for a bit when they went all soft over some of the animals, and it was very hard not to, with the newborn lambs like babies' toys, and the day-old calves like Bambis. They all went potty over one lamb which was being reared by another lamb's mother.

"That one's mother died," the girl from the farm told them. "But she's been accepted by that ewe."

"Aah! I'll have her," said Mr Brewer.

"Trust *ewe*! Get it? Ewe!"

They laughed. Mrs Winterburn was human after all: she'd cracked one! Everyone laughed except Kim – because in spite of herself she was having another of those sudden quiet moments; it was as if she was walking into them. She really didn't dwell on things as a rule – she got on. She worked hard at school and she worked hard at home downstairs in the take-away. Bed-time for her was never for staring at the ceiling and thinking about things, it was head on the pillow, turn over and sleep – usually in seconds. This week was turning out different, though: this week, standing and staring were part of the programme. And for her it was standing and staring and remembering . . .

Her mother had died, on the mother boat. Like the little lamb, Kim had been left to someone else to get her over those first dangerous days. She'd heard all about that through a thin wall, too. How, pregnant, hungry and worn out by the struggle and the strain of the escape, her mother had started having her on the boat, weeks early. How the boat had hit heavy seas and people had been thrown about and crushed in the tossing and rolling. How Kim had been born and her mother had died. And how another woman with a young child had shared her breast milk.

"Baa! You look like one of them. Don't she look like one of them, staring?" Wendy Kent was a bad enemy to make. Things went her way, or they went off. "Sheep-face!"

Big Eddie, the one Wendy was talking to, smirked his smirk. "Baa!" he agreed.

"Cleverest thing you've said all week," Kim told him. And her back stayed straight: because she was her mother's daughter, and this sort of thing was nothing to what that brave woman had gone through.

7

There was time for games that night, up on the sloping meadow they called the sports field. Organised games: football and rounders, until three rounders balls had been lost in the undergrowth on the edge and they started asking for something else. Hide and seek in the thick woods above them.

"Tomorrow, the last night," promised Mr Brewer. "Can't be late for supper twice."

They were kept waiting to go in for their meal: a bit of pay-back from the warden, probably. But while they queued, to stop them getting noisier and noisier, Mr Brewer came down the line with the letters which had come that day. And it was a very thick handful. Eyes really stared, everyone's eyes, even those of people pretending to look the other way. And there seemed to be something for everyone. For some it was the third and fourth they'd had, for Parveen it was the first – and it was the first for a red-faced Lee, whose tooth-gap smile would have made a photograph worth framing.

Something for everyone, it seemed, except Kim. At the meal table with only her plate to concentrate on, she found it hard to get her food down. All the talk around her was of London and what was going on at home; pets and grans and the telly; everyone showing this bit and that in their letters: all whispered secrets and loud jokes and ketchup on the envelopes. Debbie had got a letter from a boy she said she didn't like in the third year, written somewhere private on lavatory

paper. Pulling it out too quickly, she had to share
it with her table, every soppy page ending 'NOW
PLEASE WASH YOUR HANDS'. Mrs
Winterburn read out her husband's views on the
new council swimming pool: and Mr Brewer
tucked a letter down his jumper. But there was
nothing for Kim, not until the teachers noticed
and they found a postcard from Mr Holt for her to
be in charge of.

It gave her indigestion, her disappointment. Her
rotten dad! How old was she? How long had he
been in England? Couldn't he have put himself
out to learn enough English in ten years to write
'Dear Kim. Love from Dad' – how hard was that
to do? It was all she wanted. He could have sent

his signature written sideways down one of their menus and made her feel good. But nothing: he'd sent nothing. He was a great failure. Why couldn't he try harder and find the guts to go to classes, even if they were difficult? Why did he always have to lean on her? What sort of a rotten father was he?

"Oi! Kim – what's this say?"

It was Lee. They'd been dismissed and he had found her in the little ornamental garden with the view of the sparkling valley: the quiet place with no ball games where no-one went. He had got his mother's letter, was still grinning with it – but he couldn't read it very well.

Kim helped him. And, somehow, it helped her. In spite of her dark mood, she found herself settling into it. It was interesting how people were different. She had a dad and no mum; Lee had a mum and no dad, just uncles who came on different days. They all sent their best to him, signed their different names and put a few jokes in. Otherwise, the letter was all about the music charts and what was happening in the serials. A different life to hers. And the letter ended with more kisses than Kim could count.

There was a secret sound from the rockery above them.

"Here they are! Look at them two! Know you now!"

Kim needn't have looked to know whose jealous voice that was: Wendy – pointing, sneering, twisting up her face for Tracy. Why? She was only helping Lee, it wasn't any more than that. But before she could explain it, try to make friends again, Wendy went. She pulled Tracy away as if she had something urgent to do. Probably something nasty to Kim's bed.

"Cheers, mate." And Lee had gone, too.

The sun was casting shadows on the valley now, the sparkle had all gone from this place. Kim went to the kitchen to help Mr Brewer with the cocoa. And then she went to check her bed. But all Wendy ended up doing was to ignore it, with Kim in it. She talked loudly all round her, and was careful not to answer the couple of quiet words Kim said.

8

The next day they went to the castle at Goodrich. But their clipboards had been carried round a lot of places by then – and what really had them buzzing was the 'wide game' when they got back. Not just ordinary hide and seek, Mr Brewer promised, but something bigger, with teams and proper rules. It was to be their last night there. No diaries and follow-up work as everyone who wanted to went up to the field to join in.

Mr Brewer explained it all carefully. Half the group were to go off into the woods to hide. They'd be quite safe, he told them: the woods were bounded by a strong fence on their further side so there was no danger of anyone wandering off the site. The other half of the group would count a hundred and then go out looking for them, with a few good tacklers staying behind to guard the home base – which was Mrs Winterburn and the anoraks. Every hider who got back scored a point. Everyone who was 'had' gave a point to the hunting side. And anyone who stayed hidden till the end scored half a point when the three whistles sounded.

Those were the rules, and Kim was herded by Mr Brewer's arm into one of the groups of prey. She didn't play out of doors much where she lived, her father wouldn't let her, so this was something different. When the whistle went for the start, she ran off fast with the others, high-stepped in her wellingtons through the stingers and the fern, and quickly decided on a course of her own to the left. Everyone who went together would get found together, she reckoned. She could get a point on her own. With a quick look back over her shoulder to check who was watching who, who was going where, she disappeared into the darkness of her side of the woods. But already her heart had sunk – because what she had seen when she looked round was Wendy and Tracy and Big Eddie coming out to the edge of the group that was left, on her side of the field. So! Her new enemies were going to be her hunters.

They weren't pointing, they weren't showing by

anything very much which way they were looking, but Kim knew very well who those three were going to come after: it was definitely going to be her. She was their target, she was going to be their prey. And who would care about the rules? The real idea, what they'd really be after, was to find her, and get her and hurt her – accidentally push her over in the nettles, something like that. She knew from the way they'd been standing – all casual and pretending not to look, but smiling – that hurting her was what their game was all about.

She ran hard through the moist and slippery wood, quickly decided to go off the wide path onto the narrow track. Then off the narrow track into the undergrowth till she was crashing through tangles of bush and spiders' webs that had had nothing come their way for a year. The voices of the other hiders went distant as she looked desperately for a place well away from where Wendy might look. All she could hear as she jumped and pushed was the thump of her heart and the sounds of the fears in her head. She didn't want a quick run-in. The last thing she was after now was a point. All she wanted was to stay hidden and to get safely back to supper without any kicking or punching or scratching or stinging: without any of the things those others were out to do to her.

Cleverly, it struck her as she ran that her best protection might be the very thing she was frightened of: nettles and thorns. If she didn't like them, the hunters wouldn't either, would they? Getting tired now, legs heavy in her boots, she saw what she thought might do. Coming at it by a roundabout way so as not to show where she'd

gone in, Kim crept and crawled and weaved
herself into the biggest blackberry bush she could
find. A blackberry bush very dense and prickly, a
careful hiding place where she daren't move once
she was lying there because to move would be to
scratch herself badly. She lay there, thought of a
million better places the way hiders do, but knew
she had to stick with that one. And like that,
trembling, Kim waited.

And lying there, not thinking about anything
but her fear, she knew for sure what it had been
like on that island in Vietnam. Not from the
stories she'd heard when her father told his
brother, but from being pressed against the earth
right here. She could have been her father, and
these hunters could have been the North
Vietnamese soldiers brought south to stop him
getting away from that island, searching the jungle
with orders to capture or to kill.

She could have been her father lying there, his
wife beside him, both scared to death in the pitch
darkness. The soldiers wouldn't be blamed for
killing, these guards crashing through the foliage
with their weapons out to use.

"We're right here! We know you're there! Give up! Come on, give up!"

"Can you hear us? It's you we're coming for!"

Was it bluff? Mental warfare? Which way were the footsteps coming?

9

As she'd hoped they wouldn't, but dreaded they
would, they came her way. Wendy Kent and
Tracy Sargent came with a grudge against her
over Lee, bringing Big Eddie with them to do
what they wanted. And from their voices when she
heard them in the distance, she knew she'd been
right over what they were about.

"Snobby little dilk!"

"Show-off! Anyhow, all sorts happen when you
fall over!"

"Yeah, bad luck, eh?!"

They laughed, looking forward to hurting her.

"Only be her word against ours!"

And then it was Wendy in a witch voice with
the worst of hide-and-seek scares, calling out. "We
know you're here! You can hear us, can't you?
We're coming to get you!"

Kim didn't move. She couldn't be sure how well
she'd tucked her left foot under the bush behind

her, but she knew she couldn't shift it. She couldn't make a movement, not run the risk of a sound. They were getting closer now, only metres away; they'd done horribly well to follow her trail. She could hear their breathing, could almost feel their strong will to find her and hurt her. In despair she clawed her fingers into the cold soil, allowed an insect into her ear, stopped breathing normally and took shallow breaths which wouldn't move her back. It wasn't what she wanted to do.

She wanted to jump up and scream. Instead, it was a fight to stay still. But she fought hard, made her eyes know the sight, her nostrils the smell, her mouth the taste of the earth she was pressed so hard against.

"You hear us, Kim Lung? We're gonna get you!"

Closer. Very close. A sudden risked move, the lift of an eye. And the sight of the toe-cap of a boot so close the stitching could be counted. A cringe, a wait for the shout, for the blow – but holding the breath, fighting not to panic.

But it would only be a fist, or a boot. It wouldn't be a bayonet. It wouldn't be what her father had had: a bayonet stabbing down into the dense foliage and into his hand, into the flesh between his finger and his thumb; pinning him to the rotting earth while still he didn't shout; holding it, twisting it, then pulling it away to be stabbed into the next big plant – only the darkness hiding the blood on the soldier's bayonet.

Kim's heart beat enough to lift her body from the ground. She closed her eyes again, did her screaming inside her head, like her father had done.

And then suddenly it wasn't a scream but a whistle which sounded, three blessed times. And crashing away on a run-in from some distant place of his own came Lee, whooping in a winning way.

"Didn't get me! Half a point, I got!"

"Stupid game!" said Big Eddie. "Get a football

out, eh?"

"Yeah – when I got me half a point!"

The two boys went off: so did Wendy and
Tracy, after one last hard look round.

"Thought she'd come this way."

"Done a double back."

"Yeah. Leave it."

They ran off. But it was a very long time before
Kim could emerge. It seemed to take her a lifetime
to come crawling out of that hiding place.

10

When the coach drew up at the school everyone
on the pavement waved as if it were a royal visit.
Dogs had come, and push-chairs with little
brothers and sisters. Mr Holt, the headteacher,
was there, smiling a welcome. But it was the
parents' faces everyone wanted to see. No eyes
were ever sharper than in that first look along
Dockside for the people they lived with.

Kim, too: eyes sharper today than anyone's. And
he was there, her father, smiling shyly, waving his
hand in a small and private way. Kim saw him
and didn't push to be first off the coach. She
didn't need to. He was there, everything was all
right, she could wait. She looked out of the
window as she queued in the aisle, and she waved
again. Back came another smile, an ordinary smile,
a smile with nothing of an apology for not writing,
just pleased to see her.

She blew him a little kiss. Well, it was her fault,

too, wasn't it? She'd worked it out last night. She hadn't bothered to translate that bit about the letters, said at the end of the meeting. She'd had enough by then – so how was he to know? And she hadn't thought she'd *need* a letter from him. She could easily have left him with a couple of envelopes already addressed: but she hadn't thought she'd miss him.

At last her turn came. She jumped off the coach and surprised him with her hug, almost pulled him over. He hugged her in return and took a step back, shook his head at her. Well, why should he understand this loving? He wasn't to know this was her secret way of saying sorry for those bad thoughts she'd had about him. He wasn't to know what she knew now – that he wasn't a man of words and writing, but a man of action. A brave man those years ago, and a strong man now, a good example of how they all had to be in London. No-one remembered what had happened in Vietnam any more: no-one seemed to know, even, or to care.

But Kim did. She understood it now. And as they walked to the bus, she made sure he had her case in his good hand, and she changed places on the pavement, to get a tight hold on his bayonet scar.

GETTING IN

1

Sam Powell called it his 'office', but it was no
more than a bookcase by his chair with a short
curtain covering the front. He kept his football
pools in it, and a pen, and a magnifying glass. In
the old days when he'd been allowed to smoke,
he'd kept his makings there, too: his packets of
fly-away paper and his Golden Virginia. And
along the side of the top shelf, on a level with his
shoulder when he was sitting down, was his old
tin whistle.

It was a rare treat for Kenny when the
television wasn't on for the old man to slide out
the tin whistle and blow off the fluff and dance
his fingers along it in a bygone tune. His eyes
would burn with young pride again as he played
one of his favourites — and Kenny always knew
that it wouldn't be long before the old stories
started coming out, like readings in between the
carols. Stories of London in the war, of people

and streets that used to be, of the school when it was a fire station; of how, instead of sea shells and stamps, the children collected twisted bits of bomb and shell called shrapnel. And of the 'office' itself, which miraculously survived a direct hit on their house and had gone everywhere with Sam Powell since.

Tonight though, this Sunday night, Kenny wasn't so easily lifted. He'd have sooner stared at the television set and thought his thoughts than have to talk to anyone, even his grandfather: because Dean, his best friend, had left the school on Friday to go off somewhere with his mother, and tomorrow was a day he was wishing wouldn't come. Tomorrow Kenny would be one of those kids on their own, with no partner for anything, no-one to run around with, no mate. He'd been so thick with Dean he'd needed no-one else, and now it would be like being someone new. Especially with his problem.

The tune finished suddenly: the tin whistle went down. "You've got that *school-tomorrow* face on, boy. Not queueing up for the stick, are you?"

Kenny shook his head. It was detentions and

exclusions these days, not the cane.

"Every morning regular, no chance to give no excuse. 'How many?' – and you had to tell the headmaster what the teacher said, two or four or six. And then, swish and swish, and down to the taps to run the water on your poor old hands." The old man laughed and lifted his tin whistle to his lips, played a little scale with his nimble fingers – as if to show no permanent damage had been done. "Don't know you're born these days ..."

2

It was still the same building. The school. In all the vast space they'd cleared for the flats after the war, they had left the old three-decker standing. Dockside. Dockside Street, it had been called in Sam Powell's day, and there was still a white stone gateway with BOYS chiselled in it, and one with GIRLS, but no-one took any notice of what they said any more. The teachers went in through a gate marked BABIES. But Kenny always went in the near one, BOYS, where he met Dean every day. Where he *had* met Dean every day ...

Kenny walked past his grandparents' block to get to the school: and he suddenly felt nostalgic this Monday morning, even for the night before with his grandad and the old tin whistle. But he pushed the feeling out: there was no room for that. No, he had to keep on going. You couldn't forever think about yesterday, he told himself, or last Friday. This morning he had to face up to no

Dean, and to his big problem: to having to hear all the others now when they called him by some other name. Like Titch. Or Shorty. Or Tiddler. Or Midget. Because it was only Dean who called him Kenny all the time: Dean and the teachers. To everyone else he was one of those other names, and mostly Titch. But that hadn't really mattered much before, because Dean had been there, Dean had been his mate. And Dean had been rare. He'd been his mate since Nursery, and he'd never once made a joke about Kenny's size. It had never seemed to matter. Now Kenny was going to have to get used to not being Kenny anywhere outside the classroom. And to save himself from being left leaning on his own against a wall, he was going to have to worm his way into one of the gangs: paying the price and not minding all the names, but getting in. It was that or turning his back like he had when Dean was there; but being on his own all the time.

It wasn't a little bit funny, being small. People said things to him like, "When you gonna grow up?" or "Stand up, can't you? – Oh, you are standing up!" or "Can't you stretch him?" to his

father. And these were the adults, laughing like comedians at the London Palladium. Always the same old lines with the same old insults while Kenny stood there looking up their noses and trying to smile. And knowing that if he dared answer back, "What a big nose!" or "Wotcha, Baldy!" he'd get a wallop from his mum and no treats for a week. Being small for his age was like wearing a badge which said, "Have a go at this one! Easy laughs – don't have to be funny!" And the only way he could take off the badge was to stay sitting down all the time.

Kenny knew he'd got a lifetime of it, this being small: but it hadn't been so bad with a real friend like Dean around.

At first he hadn't known he was smaller than the rest: it had taken some time for him to know it was just him in his class. At the Nursery and the Infants everyone had been small, and everyone older had kept saying how little everyone was: they were *all* the tinies or the babies to the adults, all titches to the juniors. But when the other titches had started saying 'Titch' to Kenny he had become aware that he was still down here, sort of thing, and they were all up there.

Perhaps it was the same being fat, or black, or extra tall, Kenny thought. Or all-round big, like Big Eddie. People loved picking out differences.

3

In a way, though, while Kenny *was* small, Big
Eddie wasn't that big. He wasn't really tall, and
he wasn't really fat. What he was, was tough: and
without a doubt he was the one to get in with if
you hadn't got a special friend. His was the best
gang. Everything happened round him. He was in
the same class as Kenny and he was always where
the laughs were, because people enjoyed the fun
the tough ones made.

And that Monday it was Big Eddie who Kenny
saw first as he went in through the gate. He had
the usual crowd with him: Paul Brewer and Neil
Gull and the hangers-on. Not a lot of smiles, but
plenty of noisy laughs. Kenny watched them
mucking about with someone's plastic lunch box,
throwing it to one another, kicking it along the
playground. His inside twisted: he felt sick, and
jealous. None of them had been awake all night
worrying about coming to school today.

"Here y'are – over here!" Kenny shouted, running over, hoping to get a catch of the lunch box.

But none of them even seemed to see him. They went on teasing the kid who owned it till the whistle went. Then, pushing each other, they left the box where it was and went to line up.

It was miserable having that empty space next to him in the classroom. Friday there'd been someone there: but now it was only empty space: the chair tucked under and just a column of pencilled working-out on the formica table top to show where Dean used to sit. Kenny could remember him doing it: and, dear old Dean, it was wrong!

But, no, he mustn't look back. That was for old people like his grandad. Kenny Powell had to move on.

And at that moment luck seemed to take a hand. Big Eddie had played up or said something, and Dean's empty chair was an ideal place for the teacher to send him to. His book came first, slung on the top, then his pencil – who cared if it broke? – and then the tough kid as he pushed himself in, his elbow well over half-way on the table. Kenny gave him room; everyone did, with Big Eddie. And his pencil *had* broken, he couldn't even begin to make a start, so Kenny found him a spare from the shelf under the table.

"Get lost, Midget!" The boy pushed the pencil away, folded his arms, didn't want to do his work, was looking for an upset with Miss Barker.

"I saw that! Pick it up! And apologise to the boy next to you." Miss Barker came in once a week; she didn't know the names of the quiet ones, but she could definitely shout.

Big Eddie pulled off the impossible. He did what Miss Barker said he had to do while still making it look like he was disobeying. He grabbed up the pencil and threw it on the table. "Sorry." But it had the throat of a threat, and Kenny's inside felt like his grandad's must have, facing the cane. Because he knew how Big Eddie loved a grudge, and here he was sprawling like a wrestler between rounds, spitting on a dirty finger and rubbing Dean's marks away.

4

Kenny got home in one piece. He found a library job at playtime and he joined the choir in the dinner hour, just in case, tagging on behind Nicola Ward and some others when they went in. Yet he hated himself for feeling afraid. When his grandad came round for the pools money that night he could hardly find a word to say, went off to his room rather than sit there being moody.

The old man was nobody's fool, though, and he went in to where Kenny was lying on his bed. He rested his hand on his pillow and found it damp.

"You washed your hair, boy?"

"No."

"Been crying?"

"Yeah ... bit my tongue."

"Let's have a look."

The big light went on, and Kenny had to put out his tongue, with nothing wrong with it.

"Can't see nothing."

"An' I caught my finger in the door."

But Sam Powell's face said he knew he was hunting for Scotch mist even as he looked.

"You wasn't yourself last night, neither, boy. You sure you're not in trouble at school? Not been up to something?"

"No!"

Kenny knew his grandad wasn't the sort you fooled for long. He'd give a little look which told you when a lie hadn't worked: he'd open his eyes wide and press his mouth shut extra tight. He did it now – although he had no cause; Kenny wasn't in trouble in the way he thought.

"You can tell me, boy. You won't surprise me. There's nothing much new on this earth." The old man sat on the side of the bed and looked at Kenny kindly and definitely not going away till he knew.

So Kenny found himself telling him, in a low flat voice, very matter-of-fact, about wanting in: but being scared of Big Eddie: and about being too small to do much about it.

"Small? Course you're small. Keep telling you

– I'm small and your dad's small, and your mum's no Big Ben, neither. There'd be questions asked if you wasn't small. Can't change that, boy. But doing something about it, that's different." Sam Powell had got up and was over standing against the door: with a fair gap between him and the top of it. "Told you there was days I never wanted to go to school, didn't I? And not just on account of the stick, neither. There's always been big 'uns, boy. But over the years I found out what I was and what they wasn't."

Kenny screwed up his eyes. What was coming out now? What secret weapon did his grandad have?

"Now, what shall I tell you?" The old man thought for a moment, frowned, then cleared his brow as he made up his mind; suddenly clapped his hands like someone selling a bargain on a market stall. "Small and sharp, that's what I was. Quick on my toes and quick in here." He tapped his bony forehead with a bony finger. "We're the fast ones, boy – funny with it, it's natural for small people. Make 'em laugh! They never hit you while you're making 'em laugh."

Sam Powell stood under the light, put his
thumbs in the pockets of the suit waistcoat he
wore over his old dress shirt. "Used to do a turn
round the Working Men's Clubs, me. *Sam Spam.*
That's where I needed my penny whistle – to get
me off at the end." He did a little pose as if for
applause: his old eyes twinkled and his false teeth
sparkled. "Most of the real goers in this world
have been small," he said. "So you be a goer, boy
– and be a funny one."

5

When the light had gone out Kenny lay there and imagined himself being a goer – and a funny one. He'd always made Dean laugh, and Dean had always made him laugh: but that had been over silly imaginary things, not the stuff you could do with people who you didn't know. You needed real jokes to be funny outside your own silly sayings: and Kenny couldn't think of one single joke he'd ever heard. He racked his brains to remember, and he tried to make some up. But, nothing! He got hotter and hotter in the bed. He couldn't think of anything.

He put on his light and got up to find some paperback joke books. But as he read them through his spirits sunk lower and lower. So much of this stuff never fitted, he thought. Or it just wasn't funny. These were all things for smart little kids to say to people who'd heard them before and who only laughed to be kind. They didn't *get* you, all these things about elephants and policemen and flies in soup. Big Eddie definitely wouldn't bust a gut and want him in his gang with any of this rubbish!

But the way his grandad had stood in the light by the door had impressed Kenny. Perhaps the secret of being a goer wasn't so much in what you said as the way you said it, the way you felt inside. Grandad had really seemed the part, Kenny thought, the way he'd put on a cheeky look, smiled, bent his head in a cocky sort of way. Perhaps if he changed from being the quiet kid he'd been with Dean to someone more flash, he'd seem the part, too – and then they'd want him to be one of the gang.

He lay there and practised just being a fast talker. He thought of the ordinary things he usually said, then he imagined saying them in a more flashy way. Like, putting up his hand for school dinners, and instead of saying, "Staying," he could say, "Poison, please Miss." Things like that. It might not sound like him: the things he tried mostly ended up sounding American: but he'd be being this new character, wouldn't he?

He tried them out on the dogs and cats he passed on his way to school the next morning. All the cats did was stare as if he was barmy and one

of the dogs just cocked his leg. But it was all practice, it all gave him confidence to try to be a goer like his grandad. Sam Spam? Well, he could be Kenny Henry, or someone like that: he could be the new one of what his grandad had been, back in the old days.

He gave Big Eddie a miss in the playground; kept very quiet out there. He needed some time to impress him in the class before he went trying to get in with him outside. The dinner register would be the first chance. After the attendance check it would be the first opportunity to say anything out loud. And he'd practised for that.

He was very nervous. Mrs Winterburn wasn't soft like some teachers. Most of the younger children in trouble would sooner get sent to the Head than to Mrs Winterburn. But then you had to take a chance, being a joker, Kenny reckoned. And it would definitely show Big Eddie how Kenny Powell could be one of the lads.

It seemed to take a year for his name to be reached. It was quiet reading all round the room: mostly quiet, just the sound of Gull and Brewer changing their books every couple of minutes, and time goes very slowly in the quiet. It seemed all day, a thousand breaths before Mrs Winterburn eventually got down to his name on the dinner register. "Kenneth Powell?"

Now! And suddenly Kenny didn't want to say it. Suddenly it seemed all wrong. It sounded a crazy thing to say, as if he were someone else sitting in some different school: not Kenny, not in Dockside at all. Well? He looked up; and she was waiting for him. Should he or shouldn't he? His stomach flipped, it would need a kick to get him going. Till a quick picture came into his head of his grandad trying to help him – of Sam Spam standing by that bedroom door, smiling: and in a crazy loyal sort of way Kenny found himself saying it for the old man.

"Poison, please Miss."

Mrs Winterburn's head cocked. So did the heads from most of the class: everyone's except Big Eddie's and Gull's and Brewer's, who were deep in something else near Brewer's desk and hadn't even heard him. But Mrs Winterburn had, or she thought she had ...

"What did you say?"

Kenny met her stare, tried to look a mix of innocent and cheeky, did a little angle of his head like his grandad had in the bedroom. But, doing it, he could see Big Eddie and the others still giggling over something else. They hadn't got the first idea what he'd said. He was suddenly scared: because he wasn't the sort to be cheeky to teachers, which is what it would come down to now: that wasn't what his grandad had meant at all.

The trouble was, he didn't know how to get out of it. And still Mrs Winterburn was ignoring the rest to make him say again what he had said before. "Eh? I said, 'What did you say?' "

But Kenny's mind, his sharp-shooting quick-with-it Jack-the-lad mind had gone blank. He couldn't think of any way out. Nothing sharp and lively came to save him now.

"He said, 'Present', Miss."

"Ah."

Kenny looked round. It was Nicola Ward who

had spoken. Now it was her doing the innocent staring at Mrs Winterburn.

"Kenneth, I already know you're here. This is for dinners."

Kenny flapped at his book to show how engrossed he had been. "Sorry; dinners, please, Miss."

"Thank you." And after a long and heavy stare Mrs Winterburn passed on to the next, while Kenny looked round at Nicola again, who was head-down in her own reading.

He gave it up. He gave up being a joker there and then. It wasn't his style: it definitely wasn't, not if he had to be dug out of trouble by Nicola Ward. He skulked inside at playtime, pretending to finish off work, and at dinner time he stayed out of the way at choir again. Nicola was there: he spotted her straight away: but he didn't get a chance to say thank you. He stood on his own and tried to get into the singing. Not into it enough, though, to silence the playground noises which carried the threat — and the attraction — of Big Eddie and his gang outside.

6

"How's it going?" Sam Powell's eyes were lit up waiting for the answer he wanted to hear.

"Cracked it, have you?" He was sunning himself on a pensioners' bench, next to one of his cronies. Always smart – he went to the paper shop as if it were church – he fluffed up the hankie in his top pocket, sniffed, stared his old blue eyes at Kenny.

"Nah – not my style."

"Ah ..." The old man nodded slowly.

It was a shame to disappoint his grandad, Kenny thought, but there was no sense in telling lies. Now he felt awkward, didn't know whether to say more or run off home.

"Wassup, Tiddler? You got a face like the underside of my foot." Sam's friend, a tall sad-faced man with silver stubble, took his wet eyes off the passing traffic and stared them at Kenny. And to Kenny's embarrassment, Sam Powell started telling him.

"He wants in with the big lads," he said. "Lost his best mate. Wants in with the gang."

"Is that it?" The other old man nodded. "Wants to run with the 'ounds ..." and he went back to staring at the traffic. Kenny made to go. Then, "Bantam weight," the old man suddenly said, and he shifted on the seat, came to life, shaped-up his hands like a boxer. "Know why they never matched the likes of your grandad with us heavyweights? To protect us big 'uns! We only lumbered round, weren't boxers at all. But

him –" he gripped Sam Powell's arm "– go on, Sammy, show him!" Sam Powell started shaking his head. "Go on, show him your old rhythm. Best boxer in the squad. Got us big 'uns every time."

Sam Powell rubbed his nose. "Wasn't going to tell him all that." But his protest against the praise was half-hearted. "His mum'd murder me!" he said with a smile.

"Well, his mum ain't here. An' she won't be in the school yard, neither ..."

Sam gave it another second: no longer. "All right, boy, watch this now." He slid forward to the edge of the bench, put his legs apart, held his body straight. He clenched his right hand up in a fist at his chin, poked his left fist out as if he were asking a question in the air; and suddenly he let go the right so straight and hard it seemed he'd go through the side of a bus with it.

"See? Good guard, and poke, poke, *smack!* Good guard, and poke, poke, *smack!* Good guard, and poke, poke, *smack!* Spark out!" He showed where his opponent would be, flat on the floor.

"Royal West Kents, we was," his old friend

told Kenny proudly. "An' Sam – champeen! They all wanted him on their side. Popular as a week's leave. A little boxer can knock six bells out of a big brawler any day of the week!" He stood up from the bench on legs which seemed suddenly younger and he got hold of Kenny with his hard and trembling hands to shape him like a boxer. "See, boy? Take a pattern off me."

The old man went on holding him while Sam Powell said it. "Up with your dukes: now, good guard, and poke, poke, *smack!* Good guard, and poke, poke, *smack!*" And Kenny was worked like a little fighting machine. "Spark out! Can't fail."

"You practise that, son. They'll soon want you one of their gang. Be falling over theirselves ..."

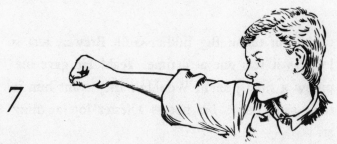

7

Kenny went home and thought about it. His
family had never made anything of his grandad
being a boxer, but he could just imagine him in
those long shorts they used to wear, with a big
winner's belt round his waist. And if Sam Powell
– who was definitely little – could do it, why
couldn't he? He'd always wanted to be able to
stand up for himself.

Secretly in his bedroom Kenny stood in front of
his wardrobe mirror and practised the stance and
the dance of a boxer. He put up his dukes and
tucked his chin into his neck, and he went
through the drill of a knock out. Good guard, and
poke, poke, *smack!* His hand shot out as if it
would pulverise the plywood door. Good guard,
and poke, poke, *smack!* It couldn't fail, he told
himself. He gave an old teddy bear what-for, and
his pillow, and clutching his new knowledge like a
gift from a godfather he went to bed ready to take

on any of them: Big Eddie, Gull, Brewer: just so long as it was one at a time. Yeah! He gave his pillow a final punch. Wouldn't they want him in their gang now? *And* not as a jester for laughing at.

He realised later that he made it happen the next day. Big Eddie took no notice of him: but Kenny was the impatient sort who wanted his life without Dean sorted out quickly.

He went looking for Big Eddie at morning playtime. He was over by a drain cover watching Paul Brewer cheating a first year out of a smart blue marble. The younger boy didn't want to play for keeps, but Brewer was having it his way.

"Course it's 'keeps'. Only play 'keeps', don' I?"

Kenny stood watching, but not for long. This was typical Brewer: and now he could impress Big Eddie by showing what he could do about it. He'd seen Big Eddie sort out Brewer himself.

"Leave him alone, Brewer. He's only a first year."

"Brought his marbles. Didn't ought to play, then."

"Not 'keeps', he said."

"Only when he lost." Brewer scooped up both marbles from the drain cover and looked round for someone else to beat.

But Kenny was standing his ground; he wasn't going to let Brewer past. "Give it back, Brewer." He said it to the boy, but with an eye making sure Big Eddie was watching this time. A quick crowd gathered, the way crowds do, ready for trouble. "You're bullying him. You wanna pick someone your own size!" While the words throbbing in Kenny's head were 'Good guard, poke, poke, *smack!* Spark out!'

"Yeah?" Brewer sneered, "Where's he, Titch?" And he kicked Kenny so sudden and so hard it took seconds for the pain to come flooding in. "Mind your own business!"

In spite of himself Kenny went down, and dropped tears on the tarmac. And when they escorted him across the playground it wasn't shoulder height by Big Eddie, welcoming him into the gang, but doubled over, helped by Nicola Ward and some of her friends, and into the medical room.

Not what he'd been after at all.

8

It seemed as if his nan was going to go for his grandad when she overheard Kenny telling him the tale. But she held her tongue, and asked him to brew a pot of tea instead, and she wouldn't let Kenny go home before she'd sat him down next to her with an old photo album she kept by her bed.

"Now just you look in here," she said, opening it with a crack. "I bet nearly every one of these was called Little Titch or Shorthouse or Midget in their day." She turned over the thick black pages. "We're a short family. But just you study this." And she picked out some of them with a crinkly fingernail. "Uncle Dougie died in the war building the Burma Road. Auntie Else brought four children up on her own. Cousin Alf from the other side of the water, butcher's boy, ended up with four shops. Edie Isle-of-Wight ran a guest house and died mysterious in Paris."

Then, just before she shut it, she found a cracked and chewed print, not stuck in. She dropped her voice. "And my brother Fred did time in prison for handling stolen goods: came out a plumber, sailed to Australia and went straight the rest of his life. Ended up head of something." Her voice was back to full strength as she fixed Kenny with an unblinking eye. "All called Titch. All done big things. And none of 'em had to run with the blessed pack."

She closed the album, just before Sam brought the tea in. "Never mind the other kids," she said, "you just be bloomin' proud to be one of us Powells."

Kenny went home thinking about it with his heart suddenly too big to go inside his shirt. She was right. Who was he to feel bad about being a titch, not being in their gang? Dean or no Dean, he'd be what his nan said – really proud to be a Powell!

9

His pride was quickly put to the test in the dinner queue next day. A pull on his arm came from nowhere while he was lining up minding his own business, and when he snapped round to see who was pulling a Powell about he saw Gull, wanting in to the queue.

"Cheers for saving a place, Titch." It was the sort of thing that happened every day. Gull barged in as if he belonged there, because all he ever needed to do to get what he wanted was to grab it.

"I never saved your place." And being who he was, fit to be fingered in Nan's album one day, Kenny pushed him back out. There were dinner ladies about to sort things if this went any further.

But that left Gull being bested by Kenny Powell. With a scowl on his face and all his strength in his twist he swung Kenny out again:

and it was Kenny trying to push back in which the dinner lady saw.

"You! Littl'un – back of the queue!" she ordered.

"It wasn't me, it was him!"

"I *saw*. Back of the queue!" Her bad-tempered face said she wasn't going to stand any argument.

"But –"

Now she shouted. "I'm not standing here arguing with you! Out!" Her arm and finger pointed. People stopped eating; a rare moment of quiet in the place.

Kenny Powell stared at her. Would Uncle Dougie have stood for that? Or Auntie Else? Or that Fred in Australia? Being made to look a naughty little boy when he wasn't? No way! He gave the woman a proud Powell look, and he went. But not out to the back of the queue. He pushed out of the hall and out of Dockside, marched across to the school gate and cleared off out into the streets, where he'd get his dinner at the fish and chip shop. Proud Kenny Powell had had enough. Why should he have to put up with all that aggravation?

10

There was a natural place to go when people were fed up. It wasn't into the estates where large and hungry dogs roamed, not into the park where other dangers prowled. It was down to the river-side walk where there were seats for sitting and being soothed, watching the high tide; and where the muddy foreshore had treasure for the finding at low tide.

Kenny walked along the narrow path and found an empty bench, tried to force a few chips down his lumpy throat. He looked out at the grey river flowing past, nothing much on it but a few bobbing sea-birds; and he thought of happier times when he'd been here. With his grandad, shaking their heads at the death of the docks opposite, staring at smart houses where cranes had used to swing. He thought of being down by the water with Dean, throwing bricks to go plunk in the mud.

Dean. Where were Dean and his mum now? Had he got a new mate at whichever school he'd gone to? Kenny knuckled his eyes in the river breeze. Because he was missing him like nobody's business.

"Wotcha."

He came back to where he was, twisted round to see Nicola Ward standing there, very awkward and ready to fly, like one of the sea-birds on land. Kenny frowned, didn't offer her a chip.

"S'all right, I'm not following you. Going home, got the dentist's."

"That should fill your afternoon." Kenny looked away, swung his legs, wished his feet would reach the ground.

Nicola laughed: but she stopped very suddenly and stared at him. "Don't get you."

"What you mean?" He screwed up his chip bag and threw it down to the water. "Joke."

"No. Being so flash. You're not you no more, you know that?"

"Who? I'm not being flash!"

"What about poison for dinner, and trying to be Superman with Brewer, and making a big thing with stupid Gull in the queue?"

"I wasn't!"

"Why can't you be like you was before?"

Nicola leant on the riverside rail, squinted at a ship coming up river to the Pool, while Kenny found himself swinging his legs more vigorously. "Why? I'm a stupid titch, push-over to Eddie and Brewer and them."

"Oh, *them*!" Nicola scorned round. "They're stupid. You're you. Kenny. There's more people around than them!"

"Yeah? Who?"

But with a swish of her skirt Nicola had turned and started walking off fast, back towards the school. Anyway, Kenny knew who she meant. Her. The one who'd saved his bacon over the dinner register.

He got up, hurried after her. "But you've got the dentist's."

"Been cancelled."

Yes! And the one who'd run the risk of coming out of school to find him and try to put him straight. What Dean would have done for him — or him for Dean.

They walked back to Dockside: Nicola hurrying; Kenny keeping up, in spite of a funny pain inside which could have been the chips.

"You're good at choir: why don't you start recorders?" Nicola asked. "Like me. Bet you'd be all right . . ."

Kenny thought about it. Why not? Perhaps he might. He wiggled his fingers like his grandad would on his old tin whistle. Yes — that seemed a Powell sort of thing to do . . .

He walked past Brewer, who didn't give him a glance. He walked past Gull who did. And he walked past Big Eddie, but by now he wasn't even bothering to look. He was grinning at Nicola, all at once feeling more like his old self; but then again feeling a bit new, in a different sort of way.